THIS BOOK BELONGS TO

_____

I am a reader and I celebrated World Book Day 2023
with this gift from my local bookseller and
Orion Children's Books.

WORLD BOOK DAY®

World Book Day's mission is to offer every child and young person the opportunity to read and love books by giving you the chance to have a book of your own.

To find out more, and for fun activities including the monthly World Book Day Book Club, video stories and book recommendations, visit **worldbookday.com**

World Book Day is a charity sponsored by National Book Tokens.

THE STRANGEWORLDS
· TRAVEL AGENCY ·

Adventure in the
Floating Mountains

L. D. LAPINSKI

Orion

By L. D. Lapinski

For Anton

whose life is littered with books

ORION CHILDREN'S BOOKS

First published in Great Britain in 2023 by Hodder & Stoughton

1 3 5 7 9 10 8 6 4 2

A CIP catalogue record for this book is available from the British Library.

ISBN 978 1 510 11183 7
ISBN (Export) 978 1 510 11196 7

Typeset in Sabon by Avon DataSet Ltd, Alcester, Warwickshire

Printed and bound in Great Britain by Clays Ltd, Elcograf S.p.A.

The paper and board used in this book
are made from wood from responsible sources.

Orion Children's Books
An imprint of
Hachette Children's Group
Part of Hodder & Stoughton Limited
Carmelite House
50 Victoria Embankment
London EC4Y 0DZ

An Hachette UK Company
www.hachette.co.uk

www.hachettechildrens.co.uk

CHAPTER ONE

In the village of Little Wyverns, it was said that the most exciting day of the year was the Maypole Festival. An uncharacteristically warm weekend had come with it on this particular year; the sun lighting up the bunting-decorated marketplace and melting ice creams faster than anyone could eat them. The maypole itself, a five-metre-tall blue, red and white striped stick, had been planted in the middle of the park like a weird alien tree.

Flick Hudson and her family were meandering through the crowds in the marketplace, browsing the stalls that had been put up for the festival. There were home-made soaps (that smelled of goat), home-made cardigans (that felt like goat), and home-made cakes (that looked like something a goat might have left behind). A sound system was letting out the occasional fuzz of static that might have been music if it was working properly. Wasps were feasting in the bins, buzzing louder than the speakers.

Flick concentrated on her ice cream, determined to eat it before it ended up down her sleeve. Her little brother Freddy was in his pushchair, wiping his own melting cone all over his face like it was sunscreen. It was the first time the Hudson family had been to the Maypole Festival, and although it seemed a bit boring to Flick, some of the older Little Wyverns locals looked as though they were about to explode with excitement.

'There's a Punch and Judy show just starting on the village green,' Flick's dad said, pointing at a smudged chalk board. 'Freddy would like that, shall we go?'

'No, thanks,' Flick said, with great politeness. She'd been secretly scared stiff of Punch and Judy after watching a show at Skegness where the crocodile puppet had been just a bit too realistic. 'I've got better things to do than watch Mr Punch and his sausage-antics.'

Her dad laughed. 'All right then, meet us back at the tombola stand in an hour.'

Flick promised to do so, and waved her family off as they trudged towards the green. Her ice cream had got to the dangerously liquid stage, so she gave up and dropped it into the bin, to the delight of the wasps. She wandered over to the embankment where a small river cut through the village. There, the festival organisers were frantically trying to stop some of the dozens of toy ducks they had set up for the Rubber Duck Race from floating away downstream before the whistle was blown.

'Ghastly, isn't it?'

Flick turned with a smile, recognising the voice. Jonathan Mercator, her best friend in Little Wyverns, was suddenly standing beside her. He was holding a Rocket ice lolly and looking resignedly at the activity on the river. Despite the warm day, teenage Jonathan was dressed formally, as though he was about to have tea with the Queen, though his black wavy hair was all over the place as usual. He was sporting a trouser suit with matching waistcoat in a deep teal and his lilac shirt was punctuated by a vermilion tie, like a luminous slash down his front. Even the rims of his glasses and his shoes were the same shining shade of conker-brown. Flick herself was wearing shorts and a T-shirt – just looking at Jonathan's outfit made her feel roasting.

'How are you not sweating?' she asked. 'And more to the point, why isn't your ice lolly melting?'

'I have a system for eating them. It's taken many years to perfect. Perhaps I'll teach you one day,' Jonathan said. He bit the top off the ice lolly, then used the rest of it to point at the duck race disaster. 'Do you think they know what they're doing?'

At that moment, one of the organisers fell in the river.

Jonathan rolled his eyes as the man got up, unscathed but soaked through. 'And they call this a festival? Honestly. I'd like to show them what a *real* festival looks like.'

'Such as?' Flick pushed her curly brown hair back behind her ears.

Jonathan gave an enigmatic smile, and pulled the remaining ice off the lolly stick with his teeth. He swallowed it, then glanced about, as if checking for eavesdroppers. 'There's something happening today,' he said quietly. 'If you're able to come with me, of course.'

Flick's heart soared with delight. The truth of the matter was, Flick and Jonathan were more than just ordinary residents of Little Wyverns. They were members of The Strangeworlds Society – a secret organisation of travellers who were able to adventure to other, enchanted, worlds. If Jonathan knew of a festival happening in a magical realm, Flick wanted to be there yesterday.

'How long will it take?' she asked, remembering she had to meet her family in an hour.

'Not long at all in Earth time,' Jonathan said. 'One of our hours is equal to about a whole day there, according to the Guidebook. We'd be back here before anyone even noticed we were gone.' He toyed with his lolly stick. 'Ready for another adventure?'

'Always!'

They left the marketplace, and quickly went up the road to where the hustle and bustle quietened down, the world became more still, and The Strangeworlds Travel Agency waited for them.

CHAPTER TWO

The Strangeworlds Travel Agency was unlike any other shop in the village. For starters, most people didn't seem to remember that the old building was there at all, and even those who did hardly ever went inside. The shop, whilst calling itself a travel agency on the big red and gold sign hanging over the bay window, had nothing inside that might suggest it actually was one. For a start, there wasn't so much as a computer on the desk. Neither were there any posters of the Maldives, Tokyo or even London. What the place *did* have was one entire wall stacked floor-to-ceiling with suitcases. There were more suitcases in the window-seat, piled between the two armchairs in front of the fireplace, and even in the tiny kitchenette at the back. There were large ones, small ones, battered ones, beautiful ones, suitcases that looked as though they'd been at the bottom of the ocean for several years, suitcases that were made of wicker, cardboard, leather, and polished wood. There were seven hundred and forty-three of them, altogether.

And each one could transport you to another world. All you had to do was step inside.

*

Flick and Jonathan entered the travel agency and locked the door behind them. It was pleasantly cool inside, and Flick was grateful for a break from the sun. She smiled as she looked around, happy to be back in her favourite place. There was a half-eaten packet of custard creams on the mantelpiece, along with a synchronous of clocks all ticking at different speeds. On the shelf behind the desk lay heaps of curly-paged paperbacks, and the smell of tea-soaked wallpaper filled the air. It was heavenly.

Even though there were hundreds of other worlds to journey to, it was the travel agency itself that truly had Flick's heart. It was the *potential* of it all, the possibilities and the promise of adventure, that made her fizz inside like a shaken-up bottle of pop.

Flick had become part of The Strangeworlds

Travel Agency last year, when she had first moved to Little Wyverns. Since that first day, when she had found herself inside the shop without really knowing why, she had been on adventures around the multiverse. She and Jonathan had battled pirates, escaped the clutches of thieves, talked to trees who could talk back, and even stood on the hand of a gargantuan mermaid-queen.

'So where are we going?' asked Flick, as Jonathan climbed up onto the desk to reach a high shelf.

'The Cloud-Wish Festival in the world of Strofadia,' Jonathan said. He took down a rather beautiful suitcase in sky-blue leather with white and silver trim, jumped off the desk, and brought it over to Flick. 'I've never been but Dad has told me about it, and I've read through the Guidebook. The festival only happens once every one-hundred years, so if we want to see it, now's the time.'

'Then let's go!' Flick beamed. 'Wait – do we need to take anything?'

'Only ourselves. Oh, and a magnifier of course,' Jonathan added, patting his waistcoat pocket before pulling out a tiny brass magnifying glass. Although it looked like the sort of thing you might get out of a Christmas cracker, the magnifier was enchanted. If you had the right magical ability, then looking through it would enable you to *see* magic. The actual physical stuff, floating about in the air. When Flick and Jonathan held a magical magnifier to their eye, they saw a gold mist, sparkling in the sunlight like glittering dust. Being able to see the amount of magic in a world was very useful, and Strangeworlds Society members never travelled without a magnifying glass.

Jonathan popped the catches on the sky-blue suitcase, and a bright light streamed from within it, along with a sweet smell of flowers. A few petals, as white as snow, drifted out of the case and settled on the wooden floor of the travel agency. Flick could hear the faint sounds of music and laughter.

'Ready?' Jonathan straightened his tie.

'Always.' Flick put her shoulders back, and stepped down into the suitcase.

The world tipped over like a sand-timer, rotating so Flick was stepping downwards and upwards at the same time, the worlds blending together like dripping paintings. But Flick kept her balance, and stepped again, clambering out of the suitcase like it was a trap-door, out into the fresh air of another world.

She emerged right into the middle of a hive of activity. All around Flick there was excitement: music, balloons, delicious foody smells, flags, kites, children zipping by laughing and playing. Gnarled and ancient trees were scattering white blossoms like snow that wouldn't melt, the wind chasing the petals around Flick's ankles and up into the air. Overhead, even though it was daytime, sparkling, vivid fireworks whizzed and popped overhead, raining colourful sparks down on the many rainbow-decorated stalls and holiday-makers.

Now, *this* was a festival.

Flick grinned widely as she looked up at the bright blue sky, which was streaked with clouds that looked as thick as cotton wool. And flying between the clouds were what Flick had taken to be flocks of birds, but now she was looking properly . . .

'Are they *people*?' she gasped as Jonathan exited the suitcase to join her.

He dusted himself down, and picked the suitcase up. 'Oh, yes,' he said. 'The Guidebook says that—' He was interrupted by a pair of the fliers landing on the ground a short distance away. They were about as tall as human adults, and wearing what looked like denim dungarees with dozens of different-sized pockets all over them. Both had stormcloud-coloured hair cropped just below their ears, which were large and scoop-like. But most remarkable were the huge, grey-feathered, towering-over-their-heads *wings* that were growing straight out of their backs.

Flick knew her mouth was wide open, but she couldn't remember how to close it.

The people walked past her, chatting away to each other happily, their lowest feathers only a few centimetres from brushing the ground whilst the highest stood a good metre above their hair. The wings, even tucked in tight as they were now, were simply *enormous*, and looked strong and powerful.

Jonathan was trying very hard not to laugh at Flick's expression.

'They can fly,' she said, remembering how her face worked. 'The people in this world can *fly*?'

'Not everyone.' Jonathan nodded at a family who were all wearing what looked like sturdy backpacks in place of wings. 'But a great many people here are born with wings, because of the way the land is, see?' He led Flick up a small incline, to where they had a better view of the world around them. Flick saw immediately what Jonathan meant.

Strofadia appeared to be made up of dozens of different islands, growing out like leaves and branches of rock, all connected to a huge central trunk, the bottom of which was lost in mist thousands of metres below. With the extreme height of the central column-like structure, you could never climb between the sky islands. It was clear that the only way to get around Strofadia was to fly.

A large zeppelin drifted overhead. As Flick watched, a door in its side opened and dozens of winged people streamed out of it, flying loop-the-loops and spiralling through the air as they headed downwards to join the Cloud-Wish Festival on the ground. Flick grabbed Jonathan's hand. 'Let's go see something!'

The stalls and tents in Strofadia were decorated in shades of blue and white, with silvery glittering baubles hanging here and there. There were embroidered wall-hangings of clouds, wings, mountains, zeppelins and dragons for sale. Delicious smells wafted through the air from food stalls that were selling sugared raindrops, cups of syrupy fog and crackling bars of chocolate-coated lightning. Flick and Jonathan chose to share a serving of Snowstorm-On-A-Stick, which looked like white candy floss but tasted like creamiest vanilla ice cream. It was better than any dessert Flick had ever had, and as a bonus, it didn't melt.

Around them, the people of Strofadia were winding through the stalls, or flying above them, towards a semi-circular clearing at the edge of the gathering of tents and sheds. Flick and Jonathan went along with them.

Some people were scattered about the clearing eating things or laughing together, but a great many of them were walking to the edge of the island of rock, where the turquoise grass they stood upon dropped suddenly away. But rather than carefully approaching the precipice, the winged inhabitants of Strofadia were leaping happily off it and flying off into the sky, towards the truly spectacular sight that waited for them on the horizon.

There were three mountains in the distance. Flick could see two smaller peaks – though smaller in this case merely meant the height of a hundred houses rather than skyscrapers – flanking an enormous, snow-capped peak in the centre. The three mountains were surrounded by ribbons of cloud and Flick gasped to see the flying Strofadian people swoop and soar close to the jagged peaks. All of that might have been wonderful enough, but the mountains were . . .

'They're . . . floating,' Flick whispered, awestruck. 'The mountains are floating.'

'Wondrous,' Jonathan breathed, absent-mindedly putting more Snowstorm-On-A-Stick into his mouth. 'Absolutely fascinating.'

The mountains were floating a good four hundred metres away from the island Flick and Jonathan stood upon, their raggedy cone-like shapes rotating oh-so-slowly in the air. The smaller ones bobbed up and down like lazy corks, whilst the middle one simply turned gradually, the snow at its top trailing away from it in a sort of cold vapour-trail that wound down the rocky surface of the mountain like a sash. It was impossible. It was beautiful.

It was what being part of The Strangeworlds Travel Agency was all about.

Flick was so busy staring at the impossible floating mountains that she didn't notice how close she was to the edge of the grass until one of her trainers slipped. She shrieked, arms windmilling in the air as she tried to get her balance back. But she was too far over. She dropped forward, bracing herself for the horrible fall into nothingness.

A hand caught hold of her arm tight and pulled her backwards. 'Careful,' the owner of the hand said. 'You should be wearing a rig.'

Flick, her heart hammering so hard she could hear it, let herself be pulled back onto the safety of the grass. 'Thank you,' she managed to say as she looked up into the face of the winged person who had pulled her back from certain death.

'You're most welcome. Are you . . . visitors?' The winged person looked from her to Jonathan curiously. Now that she was close to them, Flick could see their large eyes were a burnt amber colour, and they had tiny flecks of what might have been scales or maybe the beginnings of feathers on the side of their face. Their dull thundercloud hair was the darkest thing about them; everything else, from their off-white skin to their dove-grey wings, was as pale as cloud. Like the others, they wore denim-style dungarees, but theirs were white instead of blue, and embroidered with silvery thread.

'We are visitors, yes,' Flick said. 'I'm Flick, and this is Jonathan. We're from The Strangeworlds Society.'

'Ah, the world-jumpers.' The person nodded. 'I am Sora, a Guardian of the Cloud Dragon's Mountain.' They raised their wings in what Flick thought might be a salute, before lowering them back down. 'Have you come for the Cloud-Wish Festival?'

'Yes, it's amazing!' Flick gestured at the mountains. 'I've never seen floating mountains before!'

'Well, you picked the best time to see them,' Sora said, and their voice had a smile to it, though their mouth did not turn upwards. 'Will you be staying for the Rising tonight?'

'The Rising?' Jonathan asked. This must not have been mentioned in the Guidebook.

Sora put their head to one side, just like a bird.

'Come with me,' they said. 'I'll explain. It's really rather magical.'

'More magical than floating mountains?' Flick laughed.

'Oh, indeed.' Sora's eyes sparkled. 'But first, we should get you each a rig. The cliffs around here can be treacherous – as you have discovered.'

CHAPTER THREE

Sora led them through the hustle and bustle of the festival to a quieter area, where large tents were decorated with shining cogs and gears, hanging from their ropes like baubles on strings. The largest of these tents had several signs outside that Flick couldn't read, along with fluttering flags embroidered with yet more dragons. This was, apparently, the rig-fitters.

A 'rig' turned out to be one of the large backpacks Flick had seen worn by the non-winged people earlier. The rigs looked sturdy, but they were lighter than she had expected, with thick padded straps that fastened across the chest. They reminded Flick of a parachute backpack. Each one had to be fitted to the wearer, and Jonathan had to have one with extra-wide straps to avoid constricting his chest, since he had his binder on underneath his clothes.

'This completely ruins the lines of my suit,' he complained as he looked in the full-length mirror.

'I feel like a turtle,' Flick said, the size of the rig looking ridiculous. 'If I fall onto my back I'll have to stay there forever.' There was a pull-cord on one side on the rig, within arm's reach, but they had been warned not to touch it until they were at a cliff's edge.

Sora nodded approvingly as they exited the rig-fitter's. 'Excellent. Are you ready to try them out?'

'Are rigs like parachutes?' Flick asked.

'Parachutes?'

'You know, safety devices. Big sheets to make you drop slowly if you fall from somewhere high.' Flick tried to explain.

Sora shook their head. 'No, not exactly. I'll show you how they work.' They led the two of them to a quieter area, where the blue-green grass sloped away to the edge, rather than coming to a sudden halt. Flick felt more than a little nervous. The rig on her back was so light she could almost forget it was there – she was still not sure how it would save her if she fell off the island.

Sora reached the edge of the grass, and stretched their wings out. They unfolded slowly, spreading open like the pages of a book. The feathers on the edges of their wings were long – as long as Flick's leg – but they decreased in size in the middle of the wing before lengthening again as they got close to Sora's back, then morphing into brittle scales where they met the skin. Fully unfolded, the wings were at least twice as wide as Sora was tall, and when they beat them, the force of the wind they created almost knocked Flick off her feet.

Sora was airborne at the first wing-beat, their delicate shoes leaving the ground. They hovered, facing the two travellers from another world. 'Your rigs will allow you to travel around our world,' they called. 'You must step off the grass, and activate the pull-cord on the rig.'

'They're flying machines?' Flick asked, trying to look over her own shoulder at the rig.

'You want us to *step off the edge of a cliff*?' Jonathan demanded, clearly having different concerns. 'Is there a plan for if we should plummet to our deaths?'

'I could catch you, if that were to happen,' Sora said. 'But it's unlikely.'

When Jonathan still hesitated, Sora added, 'You'll never make it to the mountain without using a rig.'

Flick gently touched the cord on her rig. She wasn't a coward, but . . . She crept over to the edge of

19

the grass and looked down. Below was simply sky.

She turned to Jonathan. 'We've done scarier things than this.'

'Such as?' He didn't look convinced, thumbing at the straps of his rig.

'Come on.' Flick nudged him. 'We're meant to experience everything the multiverse has to offer, aren't we?' She stepped backwards slightly, her heel hanging over the edge of the grass. 'Just follow me.' With a bravery she wasn't sure she really had, she jumped backwards off the cliff.

And fell like a stone.

She might have screamed, but the rushing air stole her breath and made her eyes stream as she reached for the cord, and yanked it downwards with a *CLUNK*.

There was a sudden *whirrrrrrrrrr* from behind Flick and a jolting feeling, and then she stopped falling, like she'd been caught in an invisible net. Her arms were dangling downwards, and her legs were swinging, but something was gripping her back, as if she was a toy in one of those grab-claw machines. She turned her head to see what was making the whirring sound and gasped in delight.

Four hard, dragonfly-like wings had unfolded from her rig, and were flapping away at a million miles an hour, buzzing. The rig was keeping Flick suspended in mid-air.

'OK,' she said to herself. 'Now what?'

Sora swooped down, their wings agile despite their size. They gave a soft *caw* which Flick thought was probably a laugh. 'Tilt yourself back,' they instructed. 'You'll never see where you're going like that.'

Flick tried to do so. She ended up doing several mid-air roly-polies before she got the hang of it and could remain upright, leaning back slightly as if there was an invisible wall behind her, arms out for balance. The wings of the rig were buzzing away non-stop.

Jonathan was next. He at least managed to appear dignified as he stepped off the ledge and activated his rig immediately so the wings caught him the right way up. He looked extremely uncertain. 'I'm sure there must be another way of getting around,' he said, kicking his legs and treading air like it was water.

Flick, meanwhile, was working out how to speed up and change direction. 'This is amazing,' she said, zooming upwards, and then back down. The swooping feeling in her stomach had morphed from anxiety to excitement, and she was already wondering if she could smuggle the wings back to Earth. The rig seemed to know what she was thinking, and where she wanted to go, so steering was easy now she'd got

21

the hang of staying upright.

She drew level with Sora. 'So, what's the Rising you were talking about?'

Sora gestured over one wing. 'Follow me, I'll show you.'

*

They zipped through the air as fast as birds, towards the floating mountains. Sora took the lead, whilst Flick and Jonathan buzzed along behind. Flick loved flying amongst the clouds – it was like the best sort of dream come true. It felt so freeing and joyful to spin through the sky, the ground miles below, waving at other flying people as though this was all completely ordinary.

Jonathan, on the other hand, was loathing every single second of it. He was hanging onto Flick's ankle, the suitcase swinging from his other hand, his eyes tight shut, muttering '*I hate it I hate it I hate it I hate it*' under his breath non-stop.

Close to one of the smaller peaks was a platform suspended from a large balloon. They touched down there, and Flick nudged Jonathan to make him open his eyes.

Sora pointed at the largest central mountain. 'The

most sacred moment of the Cloud-Wish Festival comes at the very end, when the Rising happens. The Rising is when the great Cloud Dragon emerges from the central mountain and flies across Strofadia, granting wishes.'

'Wishes?' Flick asked.

'Everyone in Strofadia makes wishes,' Sora said. 'But a wish in Strofadia is not just a passing fancy or an idea, it is a touchable thing. Magic, stored in a glass bead.' They reached into one of their pockets and pulled out just that – a small bead of glass, no bigger than a penny. 'This is one of my wishes,' they said. 'Whenever the people of Strofadia have a wish, they may fly here to the great mountain, and give their wish to the dragon, in the hopes it will be one of the wishes she chooses to grant. You may make a wish at any time, but the Cloud Dragon only grants wishes once every hundred years, on the night of the festival. The rest of her life is spent inside the mountain, guarding wishes and doing whatever else it is that dragons do.'

'What happens to all the magic trapped inside the wish-beads?' asked Flick wonderingly. 'The ones that don't get granted, I mean.'

'When the dragon leaves the mountain, she releases all the trapped magic. Some of this released magic helps to grant wishes. The rest fuels the floating mountains themselves,' Sora explained. 'No wish is ever wasted, even if it not granted.'

'Do people make many wishes?' Jonathan asked.

'There's no limit on how many wishes you can make, though I think people make more now than they used to.' Sora replaced their wish carefully into their pocket.

Flick watched the ribbon of snow and cloud coil around the mountain. This whole world felt impossible, beautiful. A magical mountain fuelled by wishes was the stuff of dreams. 'Why is it called the Rising?' she asked.

'When our three moons rise tonight, the dragon emerges. At that moment, the *mountain itself* rises too, fuelled by the released magic,' Sora explained. 'The mountain spends a hundred years slowly descending, and it is only on the night of the Rising that it lifts upwards again. The excess magic returns to the mountain and strengthens it for the next hundred years. Without the Rising, the floating mountains would descend too far into the abyss below, beyond hope of returning.' Sora gave a little shudder at the idea. 'If that happened, magic would be gone from our world, forever. It would be the end of flight, of our way of life.'

Jonathan glanced over the side of the platform. 'I don't suppose I can tempt anyone to some solid ground?' he asked, rather pale in the face.

Flick had to feel sorry for him. 'All right, let's land somewhere. But can we stay here in Strofadia until the moons rise? I really want to see the dragon.'

Jonathan showed her his watch, which was permanently set to Earth Time. The hands looked stock-still; they'd only been gone a few minutes in their world. 'We can stay. But I'd rather view the Rising from ground-level, if it's all the same to you.'

'Deal.' Flick jumped into the air and fired up her rig again, her dragonfly wings whirring into life so she hovered about the platform. Jonathan groaned in resignation, and did the same.

CHAPTER
FOUR

The Cloud-Wish Festival went on all day. Sora took them to the decorated dragon temple, where Flick and Jonathan saw wishes created before their eyes. The temple was carved into one of the cliff faces that opened right out into thin air. The only way to enter was by flying inside.

Within the temple, sparkling white quartz had been carved into dragon clouds, mountains and other shapes, all leading to a huge carving of the three floating mountains on the back wall, along with a dragon head with a wide-open fanged mouth that was constantly filling and overflowing with water in the centre.

This was where the people could make their wishes.

Visitors placed their hand, along with a fistful of sand into the dragon's mouth, and wished hard. When they pulled their hand back out, the sand had changed into glass, and their wish had been trapped inside the bead. The wish-makers then promptly flew away to deliver their wish to the dragon. This being the day of the festival, the temple would close to wishes as the sun set, so everyone seemed to be in a big hurry to make their final wishes for the day and there was an endless stream of flying people going to and from the floating mountains.

As the day wore on, Flick and Jonathan explored the rest of the festival. Flick tried a bar of chocolate-coated lightning, but when she bit into it there was a *BANG* and her hair stood on end (Jonathan laughed himself silly), so she decided to stick to the less explosive treats. They listened to a band playing in a clearing of thick turquoise grass, using instruments Flick had never seen before, and their music felt both sad and joyful at the same time. People were dancing on the ground and in the sky, a swirling tornado of movement reaching up into the clouds. Sora and some of their fellow white-costumed Dragon Guardians, showed Flick how to play Sky Ball, which was a bit like basketball except played a hundred feet in the air. Back on the ground, Jonathan watched cloud-sculptors turn fluffy whiteness into shapes of creatures for children to carry around, rather like balloon animals.

By the evening, Sora had found Flick and Jonathan a good seat to view the Rising from. Dozens of raised platforms were suspended in the air by balloons, and Flick and Jonathan were shown to a row at the front. Some people were treading air beside the platforms, flapping their wings occasionally to stay in one place, and others still were zooming around, apparently too excited to stay still. Flick knew how they felt. In all her adventures with The Strangeworlds Travel Agency, she had never experienced something like this. She was about to set eyes on an actual *dragon*.

As the sun went down, hundreds of glass lanterns scattered around the stalls and platforms lit up, one by one. People's bodies seemed to glow as their jewellery and toys sparkled with light. It was like sitting amongst the stars, floating past a galaxy, and Flick's heart soared.

When the final light twinkled into being, all eyes turned to the floating mountains. Even by lantern-light, they loomed impressively. Then, there was a ripple in the sky, and the three moons of Strofadia came into view from behind a thick cloud. They were simply enormous – or perhaps really close to the planet – and they rose behind the floating mountains looking larger than the peaks themselves. The dark triangles of the mountains against the circles of the moons made an impressive vista, and Flick tried to memorise it, so she could revisit this moment in her mind whenever she wanted.

'This is it,' Sora said softly. Everyone was staring fixedly out at the central mountain. 'The moons have risen, and the great Cloud Dragon is about to appear!' They were nervously clutching fistfuls of their own feathers.

Everyone went silent, holding their collective breath.

A few seconds ticked by.

Then, a few more.

Flick and Jonathan glanced at each other uncertainly. Around them, people were starting to mutter and talk, pointing at the mountains. Sora was looking around in confusion.

Something was clearly wrong.

'What's going on?' Flick asked.

'The dragon should have emerged by now,' Sora said, worry etched on their face. 'Where is she?'

Flick looked back at Jonathan. 'Do you think we should investigate?'

'Absolutely.' He pushed his glasses up his nose.

'It is actually *my* responsibility to find out what is happening,' Sora pointed out. 'I am one of the Dragon Guardians.'

'If there's something wrong with the magic, we might be able to help,' Flick said, stealing Jonathan's magnifying glass from his pocket. 'With this.' She explained how it worked.

Sora nodded slowly. 'Let us go, then.'

Flick and Jonathan fired up their rigs as Sora launched into the night. Jonathan's complaints had been silenced this time, urgency elbowing his fear out of the way. They flew hurriedly past platforms of confused Strofadians, and up towards the mountains. A number of winged people were also flying towards it. More Dragon Guardians, Flick guessed.

They landed on a platform close to the peaks. Sora started talking immediately to their friends, whilst Flick held the magnifying glass up to her eye.

She expected to see the magic moving through the air. Some worlds had more magic in them than others, and if there was a store of magical wishes inside the mountain, then magic should be flooding out of the caves like sunbeams. It ought to have looked like a ghostly ribbon or blur of gold, sparkling here and there as it twisted and turned and touched everything in its wake.

But when Flick looked through the glass, she gasped.

There was magic all right. The magic around them was wafting through the air and clinging to Sora and their friends. But the magic close to the floating mountains looked solid. The magic was *stuck* to the mountains, coating it like armour. Perhaps, Flick thought, it was trapping the dragon inside.

'The magic isn't moving,' Flick said, shouting to get everyone's attention. 'It's stuck around the largest mountain, like a case. I think it's stopping the Rising.'

Sora looked fearful. 'The magic can't move?'

'So perhaps neither can the dragon,' Jonathan concluded.

The Dragon Guardians looked at one another. 'We need your help,' one said, their auburn wings fluffing out in agitation as they talked. 'With your magical seeing-device, you may be able to see where the problem begins. Will you go to the mountain and find out what is causing this?'

Flick and Jonathan immediately nodded.

'Sora, go with them,' the auburn-winged Guardian said.

'Yes, Captain.' Sora raised their wings in a salute, and they, Flick and Jonathan launched themselves away in the direction of the mountain. Whatever the problem was, it needed to be solved, and fast. The moons were already entirely risen in the night sky, and one hundred years' worth of wishes were waiting.

*

The mountains were all still bobbing lazily in the air. Sora directed Flick and Jonathan to a purpose-built ledge on the largest.

Now that they were right next to the mountain, Flick checked through the magnifying glass again. The golden magic was still frozen in the air, as though solid, except Flick could pass her hand through it easily.

'Has the magic moved at all?' Sora asked anxiously.

'No,' Flick said. 'It's stuck, somehow.' She looked towards a tunnel entrance next to her, still holding the glass in front of her right eye. 'It seems to be coating the walls of the tunnel too,' she said. 'Maybe the problem is inside the mountain?'

'These passageways are sacred – they have not been used in centuries,' said Sora. 'But if the dragon needs our help, we have no choice.' They tucked their wings in tight close to their body, wincing slightly. 'The passages here are narrow,' they explained. 'It is difficult even for any Strofadian to get down them, but with those rigs you will find it impossible. You'll need to leave them here.'

Flick and Jonathan quickly took off their rigs, and followed Sora down a passageway that was indeed so narrow they had to shuffle down it sideways. It opened up after a few metres, just enough for Sora's wings to not brush the ceiling, though it was still very cramped. Flick had been worried it would be dark, but the mountain's rock was veined with blue gems that softly glowed, not exactly lighting the way, but making it less than completely pitch black.

'You go ahead,' Sora said, squeezing to one side for Flick to wriggle to the front of the group. 'You can look through your magnifying glass for magical movement.'

Flick held the magnifier up as she walked, the suitcase in her other hand bumping on the backs of her legs. She couldn't see anything moving at all. Magic clung to the walls of the passageway like paint.

Suddenly, there was a groan from deep within the mountain, and the three of them froze. But the groan did not seem to be coming from a living being – it was coming from the rock itself. The mountain was still turning, floating above the ground, even though the magic was covering it like a weighted blanket, and the rocks were creaking with the effort.

A few tiny pebbles cascaded down the wall.

'Look out!' Sora just had time to yell before there was a horrible creak of rock on rock, and the passageway walls started to crumble.

Flick leapt forward, throwing herself and the suitcase away from the falling stone, whilst Jonathan and Sora were trapped behind a hail of falling rocks. There was an ear-splitting *CRUNCH* and a shout of pain, and then a rush of movement as more rocks fell rapidly into the passageway, closing the gap between Flick and her friends.

She was alone.

CHAPTER FIVE

lick shook the dust from her hair, and got to her feet. She still had the suitcase in one hand, and the magnifying glass in the other. But between her and her friends was a wall of collapsed rock.

She willed herself not to panic. 'Hello?' she called. 'Jonathan?'

'We're all right,' came a rather terse reply from the other side of the blockage. Flick's heart leapt. 'Well, alive at least.'

'Are you hurt?'

'I'm fine,' Jonathan said, 'but Sora took a rock to the wing.' There was a moan of pain from behind the rocks. 'I'm going to try and move some of these stones. Are you all right?'

'Yes. I think I should keep going.' Flick peered at

the ongoing passageway. 'The dragon might have been hurt, too.'

There was a pause. 'Be careful,' came Jonathan's reply. 'Everything I've read about dragons tells me they're not usually creatures you just walk up to . . . not without risk of burns, anyway.'

'I'll be careful,' Flick promised, though she was unsure exactly how careful she could be when preparing to face a dragon in the middle of a floating mountain.

'Good luck.'

Flick nodded, though she knew Jonathan couldn't see her, and set off down the slender corridor of rock, towards the unknown.

*

She had only walked a few minutes more before the temperature dropped dramatically. Flick's breath fogged in front of her face, and she could feel droplets of icy water on the stone walls. It felt like walking through a cloud. That gave her hope – if the dragon was a *cloud* dragon, her home might feel like this. Perhaps she was getting close.

She was right. A moment later the walkway opened up wider, and the glowing veins in the rocks brightened to reveal . . . not a dragon, but heaps and heaps of tiny glass beads. They were piled higher than Flick was tall, threatening to spill into the corridor, rolling and skittering down the glassy slopes here and there.

'Wishes?' Flick scooped a handful of them. They were indeed the same magical glass beads she had seen being created in the temple. She carefully put them back down. Was this where the wishes were guarded? In which case . . . where was the dragon?

'Hello?' Flick called, nervously. 'Is anyone . . . anything . . . there?'

For a moment, there was nothing. Then, there was a shifting in the pile of beads as if something was moving beneath them, like a cat under a blanket. Beads rolled over themselves, and Flick tried to make sense of the shape that was attempting to come to the surface. She stepped back, letting her eyes get used to the gloom, and finally took in just how big the cavern she had stepped into was.

It was several times larger than the hall at her school, higher and wider in all directions. The blue-glowing veins in the rock illuminated swathes of magical wish-beads, heaped up beyond count. The beads were stacked highest on one side of the cavern, blocking the left wall almost entirely, as much of a barrier as the rock-fall that had cut Flick off from Jonathan and Sora.

The marbles of glass in the centre moved again, this time shakily, and Flick gasped as the face and head of the dragon came into view. The head alone was enormous – the size of her family's car at least. She traced the creature's body under the pile of beads. She could see that it was coiled up, but its mass was immense. Fear shot down Flick's spine, and she realised she was trembling.

The dragon's head was round and slightly squashed, like a Persian cat's. She was a pale blue-white in colour, and the scales on her face morphed to whisker-like feathers at the sides, and a sort of feathery mane at the back of her head. She had no visible ears, but when she lifted one eyelid to stare at Flick, her eyes were a sharp shade of lilac, with a diamond-shaped pupil that flexed in the dark.

Flick stood frozen to the spot as the dragon glared at her. The reptilian eye looked her up and down, as if considering her for consumption. Then, the dragon opened her mouth, revealing thin, needle-like fangs, and spoke.

'You are not of this world.'

It was a relief to Flick that she wasn't being asked if she went well with ketchup. 'No. I mean, yes, I'm not,' she said, nervously. 'I'm Flick. I've come to help you, if you need it.' It felt important to tell the dragon this last bit as soon as possible, in case she was still deciding whether or not Flick was edible.

The dragon sighed, and from her mouth came great billows of icy cloud that swirled around the cavern like ghosts. One gust flew past Flick. She reached out to touch it, and found that – unlike the water vapour she had expected – this cloud-ribbon had body to it. She left a hand-shape imprint on the white swirls.

The dragon merely stared thoughtfully at Flick as the cloud dissipated. There was a long silence, which felt colder than the cloud had done. Flick tried to see if the dragon was injured, but she was so covered in wishes that it was hard to tell.

'The Strofadians are really worried about you,' Flick finally said, hesitantly. 'You haven't come out for the festival like you usually do. Are you hurt? Can I do anything?'

The dragon gave another long sigh. 'Every one hundred years,' she said, her voice a soft sort of snarl, 'I wake from hibernation and summon the strength to break the wishes and release the magic. I have done this for millennia, since flight began.'

'What's wrong this time?' Flick asked.

The dragon inched her head to look at Flick with one eye. She bared her teeth. 'The Strofadians' wishes have *weight*. Each wish is a want,' she said, the glass beads trickling down her body as her voice vibrated. 'And the volume of wants has never been so great. The people of Strofadia want, and want, and *want*. They pile endless wishes into my cavern, beyond even the strength of a dragon to break. I am being crushed, little one, by the weight of their demands.'

Flick put a hand to her mouth. Of course. There were thousands, maybe millions of wishes here. The Cloud Dragon was covered in them – she could barely move. Flick looked around desperately at the gigantic heaps of wish-beads. 'There must be something I can do.'

The dragon released another roll of thick cloud. 'Unless you can remove these beads, away from this cavern, so I can be free . . . there is nothing you can do. You must tell the people that the mountains will fly no longer. That magic in this world has come to an end.'

Flick shook her head – she could never deliver such devastating news. She stared around in panic. There was no way she could move all of these wishes. If the weight of them was holding an enormous dragon captive, what hope did she have?

Unless . . .

Flick looked at the suitcase in her hand. 'Do the wishes need to stay in this world?' she asked. 'Could I put them somewhere else, for a bit?'

The dragon stirred slightly, in thought. 'They could be removed for a time. As long as they were returned before the end of the night for me to release their magic.'

Flick nodded. 'I think I can do that.'

'Then, you must try.' The dragon heaved, but collapsed again after a moment, their breath coming hard, in puffs of grey cloud. 'Hurry, little one. The mountain is already becoming unstable.'

'What happens if you *don't* release the magic of the wishes tonight?' Flick asked, realising that the rockslide she, Jonathan and Sora had experienced must have been a first sign of the mountain beginning to lose its power.

'Without releasing the stored magic back into the world, the collapse of the mountains will lead to the destruction of magic itself in Strofadia,' said the dragon simply. 'If the mountains fall, the whole world of Strofadia will cease to be a place of flight and wonder. One day, even the memory of magic will be forgotten.'

'I won't let that happen!' vowed Flick. There was

no time to lose. Trying to ignore the dragon in the room, Flick pushed the catches on the suitcase. The lid sprang open, and the familiar warm scent of The Strangeworlds Travel Agency washed over her. She knelt down and stuck her head into the suitcase, emerging out into the shop. The place looked very still, the sunlight streaming in through the bay window warming the air. She pulled her head and shoulders back out, and took hold of the open suitcase like it was a two-handed net.

'Here goes.'

Flick swept the open suitcase at one of the piles of wish-beads. The beads fell *into* the open suitcase, crashing noisily to the floorboards of the travel agency.

'It works!' Flick wanted to laugh, but she had a job to do. She ran over to the Cloud Dragon, and began using the suitcase like a dustpan, scooping up piles of beads. There was no danger of accidentally scooping up the dragon herself – she was simply too big. The beads cascaded down into the travel agency (Flick didn't even want to think about what Jonathan would say about all this), and little by little the dragon's front limbs were uncovered.

She snarled in triumph, beginning to drag herself with three-clawed feet out of the remaining pile. 'The entranceway,' she said. 'Clear it. My strength is returning, and I must fly.'

Flick ran over to where the dragon was indicating. It was the solid wall of beads Flick had noticed when she entered the cavern, but now she was close up, she could see that it wasn't a wall at all. It was an enormous *doorway*, blocked solid with wishes. If Flick swept the suitcase into the wall of glass, she could end up buried herself under an avalanche of beads.

'Here.' The dragon, hauling herself free, dragged her body over to Flick, who noticed that the magical beast had no visible wings. 'Shelter beneath me. I will protect you from the falling beads.'

The great Cloud Dragon placed limbs the size of oak tree-trunks either side of Flick, who thought this might probably be the weirdest and most fantastical thing she'd ever done. The dragon's enormous head craned over Flick, shielding her completely. The claws at the ends of her feet were like curved black swords.

At that moment, there was a *crash* from the smaller corridor leading to the cavern. For a moment, Flick feared the passageway had collapsed entirely; then she let out a breath of relief as a dishevelled Jonathan appeared, helping a limping Sora into the cavern.

When they saw the dragon, the two newcomers froze instantly. Then, Sora dropped to their knees, bowing their head.

Jonathan gawped up at the dragon with the expression of someone who was waiting for the thing in front of him to vanish at any moment.

'Hi!' Flick waved from under the dragon's chest. 'You made it – are you OK?'

'Never better,' Jonathan muttered, still staring.

'Good. Now, we have a dragon to set free.' Flick turned back to the wall of wishes, and plunged the suitcase into it.

The glass beads immediately cascaded down into the travel agency, dropping like bullets. The dragon's head protected Flick from the worst of it, and as she let more and more wish-beads flow through the suitcase into her world, the entranceway was partially revealed. The remaining beads in the wall trembled, then collapsed in a wave of trapped magic. Flick dropped the suitcase in fright, and was swept off her feet for a moment by the tide of beads, before something firm grabbed her at the back of her T-shirt and hoisted her into the air. It was a second before Flick realised that the Cloud Dragon was holding her T-shirt tight in her teeth.

Meanwhile, on the ground, millions of wishes were pouring into the suitcase, until the blockage to the entranceway was fully cleared. Moonlight suddenly streamed into the cavern, lighting up the stone and glittering off the scales of the great Cloud Dragon.

As the tidal wave slowed, Jonathan waded through the beads and grabbed the suitcase before it could be swept away like a leaf heading downstream. Gradually, the movement of the wishes stopped, and the beads settled into the cavern – no longer blocking the exit, but still an overwhelming amount.

Sora, whose right wing looked crumpled, pulled themselves free of the wishes. 'This certainly explains why you were unable to fly with us, Great One.'

The dragon set Flick down before speaking. 'Indeed. The weight of requests had me crushed to the cavern floor. Without this girl's help, I would still be trapped beneath the uncountable wishes.'

Sora looked in dismay around the cavern. 'We had no idea. The wishes were made over so long . . . one hundred years.'

The dragon turned, her tail swishing viciously. Mist poured from her mouth as she spoke. 'Just imagine how many of these wishes might have come true in a century through a person's own actions, rather than waiting for magic to make them so! You must not turn to wishes for every passing whim and fancy, but keep them only for the most worthy desires, and those that could never be achieved otherwise.'

Sora hung their head. 'We almost lost you, and our mountains, because of our greed.'

The dragon snorted. Then she looked to the entrance. 'A hard lesson to learn. But one that shall not be repeated, I am sure of it.' She inhaled deeply, the cloud she had exhaled disappearing back up her flared nostrils. 'It is time. The moons have risen. The mountains await the spell.' She looked at Sora. 'You are hurt, Guardian.'

'I will heal.'

'Indeed you will.' She huffed out a little breath, vapour like the other, except this one seemed to glow from the inside, as though a light was hidden in the tiny cloud. The puff of light floated over to Sora, then melted against their body. Sora gasped, their amber eyes large as their wings spread open, high and wide . . . and completely healed.

Jonathan put a hand to his mouth and Flick had to clap for joy as Sora examined their once-broken wing in astonishment. Then, the winged guard flew over to the dragon and hugged one of her legs in what Flick suspected was probably not official Dragon Guardian protocol.

'Thank you, Great One,' Sora said, letting go. 'I shall fly in your honour for the rest of my life.'

'And now, it is my turn to fly.' The dragon crushed a foot down onto the piles of unsmashable glass. 'The magic awaits.' She inclined her head to Flick. 'Join me. Accept this as my offer of thanks.'

'You mean – ride on you?' Flick stammered.

'Your wingless friend, also.'

'I assume that means me,' Jonathan said, staggering over to Flick. He lowered his voice as he raised the suitcase. 'I cannot *believe* you've filled my travel agency with wishes, Felicity, this really is beyond—'

'We have to return all the wishes to Strofadia tonight,' Flick interrupted. 'Don't worry, Strangeworlds will be back to normal before you know it.'

The two of them clambered up so they were sitting just behind the dragon's head. The feathery scales were easy to grip onto, and Flick squirmed in excitement as the dragon pushed the rest of the wish-beads out of her way, and launched herself straight into the night sky.

The air whipped Flick's hair back and she hung onto the feathers for dear life as the dragon flew upwards. The dragon had no wings, but she swam through the air like an eel, winding herself around and around the central floating mountain, leaving a trail of glowing cloud in her wake. Flick could hear the festival crowds shouting and cheering as their beloved dragon finally made her appearance. Sora flew alongside them, their heavy wings beating fast to try and keep up.

The dragon wound herself upwards in a spiral around the floating mountain, and when she reached the peak, she began to glow! Light travelled from the dragon's body, out from her tail, joining the cloud vapour behind them. The white glow travelled quickly around and around the spiral of cloud, which lit up brighter and brighter, before disappearing back into the mountain-side entrance the dragon had emerged from moments before.

'What's happening?' Flick yelled over the rush of the wind.

'The spell,' the dragon roared back. 'My flight ignites the magic, releasing the power of the wishes, which enables the mountain to rise again. I can complete this flight only once a century, and then I shall rest.'

There was a *FLASH* of light from the mountainside entrance, and the white glow suddenly lit up with veins of blue electricity that shot out of the mountain and raced up the dragon's vapour-trail. The blue lightning dug into the mountains and spread like vines, wrapping the dragon and her riders in the crackling magical power as they rose higher and higher into the sky.

'Skyward!' the dragon roared, swimming upwards as the mountain too rose, racing it towards the stars.

Flick wanted to scream, but she couldn't open her mouth. Behind her, Jonathan had his eyes shut and was clinging onto the suitcase and the dragon's feathers with an iron grip. The two of them could only hang on as the dragon beat the mountain up into the sky, and they were silhouetted against the trio of moons on the horizon.

More cheering erupted from the Strofadian onlookers, who all took to the skies themselves, with their wings or rigs. The sparkling azure magic faded to a sky-blue glow that streamed out behind the great Cloud Dragon, illuminating the Cloud-Wish Festival more beautifully than any fireworks.

Flick whooped and waved as Sora flew beside them. The dragon looped-the-loop and swam through the air in joy as the magic poured back into the world, with the promise of granted wishes for those lucky enough. The illuminations filled the sky like shooting stars, and Flick knew that this would always be one of her favourite moments of her whole life.

CHAPTER SIX

Flick and Jonathan sat on the edge of the flying platform, eating the last of their Glow-Bug Pop ice lollies. The suitcase back to Strangeworlds was beside them, having been emptied of wishes not long before.

'It's strange to think of wishes having weight,' Jonathan said.

'Yes, heavy enough to weigh down a dragon,' Flick agreed. 'Still, we've seen things that are stranger than that.'

'Very true.' Jonathan finished his Glow-Bug Pop and put the wooden stick in his pocket. 'The rubber duck race in Little Wyverns, for one.'

Flick had to laugh. 'At least at home we don't have to rescue dragons to make sure a festival is a success.'

'Exactly, it's frightfully dull for all concerned.'

Flick looked around at the shimmering vapour-trails, the sparkling lights and the groups of happily flying friends and family. The children were chasing after the great Cloud Dragon and the adults were talking seriously about how the weight of their desires had almost lost them their mountains altogether, and how they would never let it happen again.

'What would you wish for?' Flick asked. 'If you had to wait one hundred years for it to come true.'

'If I live to one hundred and eighteen I think that would probably be a reward by itself, don't you?' Jonathan quirked an eyebrow.

'All right, but . . . if you lived as long as Sora, like the people here. What would you wish for, if you had to wait a century to find out if it would even be granted or not?'

Jonathan was quiet for a moment. Then, he pushed his glasses up his nose. 'Nothing,' he said. 'I think one hundred years would give me plenty of time to realise that you can't sit around waiting for a wish to make you happy.' He looked at Flick. 'What about you?'

'A lifetime supply of custard creams, maybe?' Flick grinned.

'Now, why didn't I think of that?'

They sat together, as the sky overhead became streaked with light against the dark.

Jonathan pulled the suitcase over. 'We ought to be getting back. I don't want your parents to think you've gone missing.'

'Good thinking.' Flick stood, memorising the view of the floating mountains, the air-swimming Cloud Dragon, the lights of the festival. A sight she would never forget. She might never be back to see another Cloud-Wish Festival, but there would be plenty of happiness in her own world.

She stepped into the suitcase, and out of it again into the familiar warm tea-and-biscuits atmosphere of The Strangeworlds Travel Agency. The wall of suitcases seemed to smile down at her as the sunlight glinted on their catches and locks, and Flick knew she was lucky. There was one thing she would never have to wish for.

Adventure. It was only ever a suitcase away.

THE END

ACKNOWLEDGEMENTS

My heartfelt thanks must go to the wonderful people who organise and run World Book Day. Thank you for giving Flick and Jonathan another adventure, and for keeping the doors of The Strangeworlds Travel Agency open. Giving children the opportunity to take home a book of their own is the most wondrous kind of magic there is, and long may it continue. You will be welcome to submit your Society applications, the next time any of you are in Little Wyverns.

Thank you to my editor, Lena McCauley, for the mountains. To my marketing and publicity heroes Beth McWilliams and Dominic Kingston, and my awesome designer Samuel Perrett, thank you for your hard work as always. Thanks also to Natalie Smillie for yet another stunner of a cover illustration.

My agent Claire Wilson needs no introduction,

but she does deserve a few medals. Thank you for everything, Claire.

And to my family . . . thank you for fuelling me with love.

ABOUT THE AUTHOR

L. D. Lapinski lives just outside Sherwood Forest with their family, a lot of books, and a cat called Hector. They are the author of *The Strangeworlds Travel Agency* series, and the upcoming standalone *Jamie*.

When they aren't writing, L. D. can be found cosplaying, drinking a lot of cherry cola, and taking care of a forest of succulent plants. L. D. first wrote a book aged seven; it was made of lined paper and Sellotape, and it was about a frog who owned an aeroplane. When L. D. grows up, they want to be a free-range guinea pig farmer.

You can find them on Twitter @ldlapinski or at ldlapinski.com

AT THE
STRANGEWORLDS
· TRAVEL AGENCY ·

**EACH SUITCASE TRANSPORTS YOU TO
A DIFFERENT WORLD. ALL YOU HAVE
TO DO IS STEP INSIDE . . .**

Read on for an extract of
Olive Jones and the Memory Thief,
Kate Gilby Smith's fun-filled ride with spies,
stolen memories, and a futuristic twist!

CHAPTER ONE

The Funeral of Grandma Sylvie

Olive Jones was looking through her bedroom window at the bungalow opposite. For almost thirteen years – in other words, Olive's entire life – her grandmother had lived just across the road. And now the house was empty.

Those who'd attended the funeral service had been invited to Olive's home afterwards for a hastily arranged buffet and cups of tea. Olive had filled her pockets with cheese sandwiches and escaped to her bedroom as quickly as she could. She'd wanted desperately to be away from all the gloom.

Truth be told, in that moment Olive found being gloomy quite difficult. It wasn't that she didn't feel sad that her grandmother had passed away. It was just that, well, she hadn't really *known* her. Their houses were barely twenty metres apart. And yet Grandma Sylvie might as well have lived in another country. Though she'd retired from her job as an accountant years before they were born, somehow she'd always been too busy to pop over to visit her grandchildren. On birthdays she used to drop cards through the letterbox for Olive and her younger brother Frankie with crisp ten-pound notes tucked inside. By the time the card reached the doormat, however, no matter how fast the children got to the door, she was nowhere to be seen. She'd always been invited for Christmas but hadn't ever shown up. Sometimes months would go by without a single sighting of her. Whenever Olive *had* encountered her grandmother – passing her on the pavement, say – the elderly lady would smile and then quickly rush away before Olive could do more than open her mouth. On these occasions, Olive often had a feeling there was something Grandma Sylvie wanted to say, but after years passed without her grandmother ever breaking her silence, Olive decided this was only wishful thinking.

Even so, Olive had learned a little about her grandmother over the years. Olive knew that she liked to keep informed about world events; Grandma Sylvie collected the newspaper from her doorstep first thing every morning. Olive could tell that she cared about helping wildlife, having seen how she faithfully restocked the birdfeeder in her front garden, sometimes feeding the robins straight from her hand. Olive also knew that her grandmother was exceptionally fit. On a few occasions, Olive had seen her sprinting around the block after dark. Twice she'd witnessed her using a thick tree branch for a round of pull-ups. And once Olive had seen her grandmother trip over a garden hose and turn the fall into a perfect somersault, landing firmly on both feet and walking away without even a pause. As remarkable as those occurrences were, Olive felt certain she was the only person to have noticed them. Nobody else was paying attention. In the eyes of her neighbours, Sylvie Jones was simply an elderly woman who preferred to keep to herself.

When she was younger, Olive had secretly wished for a replacement grandmother. She wanted the kind of grandmother she'd heard about. The kind some of her friends at school were lucky enough to have, the ones who liked things such as gardening and watching daytime murder-mysteries. The type who pinched cheeks and produced endless pear drops from their handbags. She would have liked a grandmother who read bedtime stories. The very thought of

Grandma Sylvie doing any of these things was frankly preposterous.

'She's just old-fashioned,' explained Olive's mother. 'She doesn't like to make a fuss.'

But Olive was far from satisfied by this explanation. As she got older, she stopped wishing for a new grandmother and instead became intensely interested in the one she had. *Why is Grandma Sylvie so secretive?* she wondered. *What keeps her so busy all the time? Why does she stay so fit and strong? What if . . . she's hiding something?*

Olive's mother had found this suggestion quite amusing. 'What on earth do you think a lady in her eighties might be hiding?' she'd said. 'Your grandmother worked hard as an accountant and these days she likes to take advantage of her well-earned retirement to travel and stay active. Exercise helps her arthritis.'

But Olive wasn't convinced. There had to be more to it. 'Maybe she likes to travel. *Or . . .* maybe she has a secret life she doesn't want us to find out about!' she'd replied.

Olive's mother laughed even louder. 'Sorry to disappoint you, Olive. We're not the kind of family who has secrets. What you see is what you get.

You have an overactive imagination.'

What you see is what you get. Well, if you asked Olive, what she saw of her grandmother was decidedly strange. As for having an overactive imagination, Olive couldn't deny *that* was true.

The thing was, Olive wanted desperately for her life to be more exciting than it actually was. She wanted it to be more like the films and TV shows she loved to watch, with their explosions and car chases and daring rescues. If you asked her to, she could recite lines from at least twenty-seven different films by heart. Olive herself, however, was nothing like the heroes of her favourite action movies. She was tall for her age, with long dark hair that annoyed her if it wasn't tucked behind her ears, and she had a slightly pointier chin than most. She was also the third-fastest runner in her entire year group, thanks to her very long legs. But by all other measures, Olive was distinctly average. With the exception, of course, of her imagination.

Olive was a world-class dreamer – growing up in a place where *nothing ever happens* will do that to a person. Any perfectly innocent creak of a floorboard was always, in Olive's mind, something much more dramatic – a gang of thieves searching for hidden valuables or a pack of vampires hunting for their latest snack. If she heard a car engine backfire when out walking with her mother and brother, Olive's mind would race straight to bank robberies and diamond heists. One time, she'd been utterly convinced that the local postman was lacing letters with poison as revenge for being chased by neighbourhood dogs. He had been quite surprised on his morning rounds to find her spying on him from the bushes. Then there was the supply teacher at school, Mr Harold, who Olive had suspected of being an escaped high-security prisoner she'd seen on the morning news. Mr Harold hadn't been too happy when Olive had confronted him about it. (In her defence, they did have very similar-looking sideburns.)

Olive's imagination was always getting her into trouble. Her school report was littered with descriptions such as 'must try harder to concentrate' or 'can't seem to settle in class' or 'often distracts her classmates'. Olive wanted to do better – she really did – but somehow, she couldn't help going that little bit too far. She was the one who set fire to her lab coat in science the very first time they were allowed to use Bunsen burners. The one who tried to climb the oak tree in the playground and got stuck halfway up, so the fire brigade had to be called to get her down. The one who *accidentally* started a rebellion when the teachers tried to ban unhealthy food at lunchtime (but to be fair to Olive, how could she have possibly predicted that her speech defending pizza would cause a food fight?).

Her biggest problem was, as much as she tried to listen to her teachers in class, Olive could never stop her mind from wandering. It didn't help that Olive's brother, Frankie, who was two years younger, was a model student. Like his sister, Frankie was tall for his age, with a head of dark brown hair that fell over his eyes. Unlike his sister, Frankie was often described as 'a shy but thoughtful student' by his teachers (and a 'swot' or a 'geek' by his less kind classmates). People were always surprised to find out who his sister was. Olive was sometimes surprised they were related too. Frankie was a proud member of both the choir and orchestra, as well as captain of the chess club, activities which kept him late after school most afternoons. (Olive often stayed late too, but in her case it was for detention rather than extra-curricular activities.) Though they'd been thick as thieves when they were younger, they rarely spent much time together these days. She'd never admit it, but Olive was a little jealous of her brother. Why couldn't she be more like him? Why couldn't she learn to behave herself?

Still – as far as Olive was concerned – just because *sometimes* she got carried away with her imagination, and *some* of her previous theories about people in the neighbourhood had missed the mark, it didn't mean that she wasn't right about Grandma Sylvie.

She just couldn't shake the feeling that there was more to her grandmother's life than she was letting on. So, for a long time, Olive held on tightly to her suspicions, perhaps because the alternative – that her grandmother didn't *want* to get to know her – was too sad a thought to accept.

It was only when Grandma Sylvie passed away from a suspected heart attack, aged eighty-four, that Olive decided the time had come to let her suspicions go. Her mother was clearly right. Olive had let herself get carried away again. There were no secrets to discover – only a grandmother she had never really known. And one that now she never would.

This realisation had stayed with Olive for the duration of the funeral, and on the ride back to their house afterwards in the long black car, and as relatives crowded into their living room and started helping themselves to pineapple on sticks. And it was all she was thinking about now, sitting on her bed, watching her grandmother's house across the road.

The bungalow itself was perfectly ordinary looking, with grey, pebble-dashed walls and white lace curtains that were always kept closed. The garden at the front was overgrown with a flaky wooden gate that swung creakily in the wind. The house felt – like Olive's relationship with its former inhabitant – both completely familiar and utterly mysterious.

Olive again wished, as she had done many times before, that she could peel back the bungalow's lace curtains and take a look inside. What would she find there? She knew she would have to go back to the buffet in the living room soon – she'd already heard her mother call her name more than once – but she gave herself a few more minutes to take it in.

Olive tried to memorise her grandmother's house. It would be sold soon, and no doubt the new occupant would change things. They'd fix the gate, and replace the old-fashioned curtains, and weed the garden, and in so doing, take away all the things Olive had grown to like about the place over the years.

She was squinting, imagining how the bungalow would look with all those changes, when something caught her eye.

A twitch of white lace.

Olive blinked, straightening up. At first, she thought her eyes must have been playing tricks on her. It had been a long morning, after all, and she'd probably eaten one too many pocketed cheese sandwiches.

Then it happened again. This time it was clear. One of the lace curtains had moved. No, it hadn't moved. Curtains don't twitch on their own accord, or not usually anyway. One of the lace curtains had *been* moved.

Somebody was in the house, Olive realised with a start. But that couldn't be. Her mother had the only key and Olive could still hear her talking in the other room. The house should have been empty.

Who could be in there? she wondered, and as she thought it, a hand appeared as if from nowhere and drew the curtains aside. Olive gasped. She uncrossed her legs and rose on to her knees. Her face was so close to the window now that her breath fogged up the glass. The truth was undeniable. Somebody was standing at the window of her grandmother's house. Not only that, but they were *looking directly at her*.

It had never occurred to Olive, in all the time she'd watched her grandmother's house, that *she* could also be watched. She jumped backwards, half falling off the bed.

Olive took a breath to calm her racing heart, and then, slowly, she returned to her place at the window. The person standing in Grandma Sylvie's house raised their hand and waved. It wasn't a wave of greeting, although that would have been strange enough.

It was, unmistakably, a wave which said . . . *come here*.

WORLD
**BOOK
DAY**
2 MARCH 2023

Happy
World Book Day!

When you've read this book, you can keep the fun going by: swapping it, talking about it with a friend, or reading it again!

What do you want to read next? Whether it's **comics**, **audiobooks**, **recipe books** or **non-fiction,** you can visit your school, local library or nearest bookshop for your next read – someone will always be happy to help.

SPONSORED BY

NATIONAL
BOOK
tokens

Changing lives through a love of books and reading

World Book Day® is a charity sponsored by National Book Tokens

Illustration Allen Fatimaharan

World Book Day is about changing lives through reading

2 MARCH 2023

When children **choose to read** in their spare time it makes them

| Feel happier | Better at reading | More successful |

Help the children in your lives **make the choice to read** by:

1. **Reading to them**
2. **Having books at home**
3. **Letting them choose what they want to read**
4. **Helping them choose what they want to read**
5. **Making time for reading**
6. **Making reading fun!**

SPONSORED BY

Changing lives through a love of books and reading

World Book Day® is a charity sponsored by National Book Tokens

Illustration Allen Fatimaharan